WALLY'S DETECTIVE BOOK FOR SOLVING PROBLEMS AT SCHOOL

Carolyn Webster-Stratton, Ph.D.

Wally's directions for parents and teachers about how to use this book

Make reading this book a fun game.
Wally's detective book will become more useful with time and repetition. This book is best read to children by teachers and parents in short intervals, perhaps doing three or four of the problems in one reading. Make the problem-solving game fun and praise the children's ideas for solutions with phrases such as, "Wow! You are a great detective. You're thinking of so many ideas." You and your child might even keep score of how many solutions you come up with on Wally's solution score card. However, the main idea is not to force children to come up with "right" answers to the problems (or the same ones as Wally) but rather to help them think about the conflict situations and then generate as many ideas as they can. It is the generation of ideas that is important.

Act out solutions.
Children also like to role play or act out their solutions. They find it fun if you ask them to show you how they would actually solve the problem. The parent, teacher or another child can play the part of the child with the problem, and several other children can act out their solutions. This acting is not only fun but it helps children better understand the possible consequences of their solutions.

For young preschool children, focus on generating solutions.
For very young children to start, you may need to suggest or model some possible ideas for solutions. You may even ask the children to draw their own ideas for solutions so that they can make their own detective solution book.

For older children (ages 5 to 8 years).

As children become comfortable generating solutions you can ask them some of the following questions to help them learn to evaluate their solutions.

- Do you think the solution is fair?
- Does the solution lead to good feelings? How would you feel if someone did that?
- Is the solution safe?
- What do you think would happen next if you tried the solution? This helps the child think ahead and anticipate the consequences.
- Is there another solution that might work?
- Which solution do you think is the best one to try first?
- If the solution didn't work, what would you do next? Prepare children for the possibility their solution may not work.

Explore feelings.

Each of the problem situations presented here evokes different kinds of feelings such as disappointment, sadness, fear, anxiety, embarrassment, frustration and anger. As you read and discuss the problem with children ask them how the characters in the story are feeling and help the children put labels to the feelings i.e., to name their feelings. Labeling feelings is key to children learning better regulation of their emotional responses. Only when children can put a word to a feeling and express it to someone else can they begin to feel some self- control over the situation.

Make it personal.

As you discuss the hypothetical problem situations and explore the feelings and possible solutions, you can ask children about their own experiences with similar problems.

- Have you ever had a problem like that or felt that way about something?
- How did you solve it?

Wally's instructions to detectives in training

Let's see how good your detective skills are! In this book Wally Problem-Solver presents you with a problem to solve. Think of a possible solution or even more than one solution if you can! Then turn to the corresponding pages in the back of the book containing Wally's solutions, and see if you had any of the same ideas that Wally had. Give yourself a point for every solution of yours that is the same as Wally's. Give yourself a bonus point if you had a different solution. See if you can earn enough points to get in Wally's detective club.

Remember when you think of a solution to ask yourself:
Is it fair?
Does it lead to good feelings?
Is it safe?

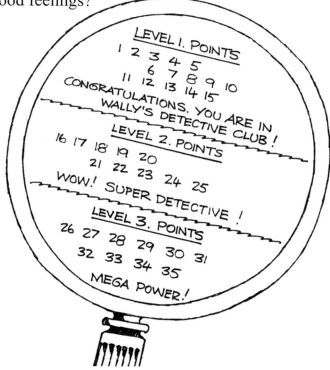

LEVEL 1. POINTS
1 2 3 4 5
6 7 8 9 10
11 12 13 14 15
CONGRATULATIONS. YOU ARE IN WALLY'S DETECTIVE CLUB!

LEVEL 2. POINTS
16 17 18 19 20
21 22 23 24 25
WOW! SUPER DETECTIVE!

LEVEL 3. POINTS
26 27 28 29 30 31
32 33 34 35
MEGA POWER!

The Problem-Solving Case 1: "I forgot."

Freddy forgot to bring his homework home and he has a reading assignment due the next day. What should he do?

Think about your own solutions and then turn to page 33 to see if you found any of Wally's ideas.

The Problem-Solving Case 2: "Pick me."

Molly Manners has her hand up because she knows the answer to the teacher's question but the teacher doesn't call on her. What should she do?

Think about your own solutions and then turn to page 33 to see if you found any of Wally's ideas.

The Problem-Solving Case 3: "I can't do it."

Tiny Turtle finds it hard to read and write. He is slow and makes many spelling mistakes. What should he do?

Think about your own solutions and then turn to page 34 to see if you found any of Wally's ideas.

The Problem-Solving Case 4:
"I want it now."

Wally's classmate, Big Red, has been using the computer for
ages and he doesn't want to share. Wally wants a turn. What
should he do?

Think about your own solutions and then turn to page 35 to see
if you found any of Wally's ideas.

Problem-Solving Case 5: "Left out."

Wally sees his friend Freddy Feelings crying, being left out of a football game and even bullied by some bigger kids on the playground. What should he do?

Think about your own solutions and then turn to page 36 to see if you found any of Wally's ideas.

Problem-Solving Case 6:
"How can I help?"

Molly knows her friend Felicity Feelings, is going through a rough time because her parents are getting a divorce. What should she do?

Think about your own solutions and then turn to page 36 to see if you found any of Wally's ideas.

Problem-Solving Case 7:
"I want to play."

It is free play time. Some kids are playing a board game and
Freddy wants to play, but they are halfway through the game.
What should Freddy do?

Think about your own solutions and then turn to page 37 to see
if you found any of Wally's ideas.

Problem-Solving Case 8:
"I'm losing."

Big Red and Wally are playing a board game. Wally is losing badly and feels like giving up. He's getting quite frustrated. What should Wally do?

Think about your own solutions and then turn to page 38 to see if you found any of Wally's ideas.

Problem-Solving Case 9: "I'm so mad."

Wally just yelled at Freddy for dropping his special model car on the floor and breaking it. What should they both do now?

Think about your own solutions and then turn to page 39 to see if you found any of Wally's ideas.

Problem-Solving Case 10: "It's not fair."

Wally is playing soccer in an important game against another school. If his team wins they'll be in first place. Wally's friend, Oscar the Ostrich, is usually 'on the bench' and rarely gets to play because he is somewhat clumsy and not as good a player as his teammates. Wally knows that Oscar is embarrassed because he is sitting on the bench so much and that he really wants to play more. Oscar has trouble speaking up about his feelings. How can they solve this problem?

Think about your own solutions and then turn to page 40 to see if you found any of Wally's ideas.

Problem-Solving Case 11:
"My friends are doing it so should I?"

Freddy's friends want him to leave the playground to go to another park. However, the teacher has told them they are not to leave the playground. What should Freddy do?

Think about your own solutions and then turn to page 40 to see if you found any of Wally's ideas.

Problem-Solving Case 12: "I'm being teased!"

Oscar is teased by a classmate and called a name for being so clumsy and shy and different from the others. What should he do?

Think about your own solutions and then turn to page 41 and 42 to see if you found any of Wally's ideas.

Problem-Solving Case 13:
"It's not fair, no one is helping me."

Molly and her classmates have been asked by the teacher to clean up the sports equipment but her classmates won't help her. What should she do?

Think about your own solutions and then turn to page 43 to see if you found any of Wally's ideas.

Problem-Solving Case 14:
"I made a mistake."

Molly spills paint all over Felicity's new dress. What should they do?

Think about your own solutions and then turn to page 43 to see if you found any of Wally's ideas.

Problem-Solving 15: "I'm accused."

A classmate accuses Molly of cheating on a game. What should she do?

Think of your own solutions and then turn to page 44 to see if you found any of Wally's ideas.

Problem-Solving 16:
"My teacher is mad at me."

The teacher yells at Big Red all the time because he has trouble paying attention and often daydreams. What should he do?

Think of your own solutions and then turn to page 44 to see if you found any of Wally's ideas.

Problem-Solving 17:
"She won't give it to me."

Molly wants to read a particular book, but Felicity is reading it and won't give it to her. What should she do?

Think of your own solutions and then turn to page 45 to see if you found any of Wally's ideas.

Problem-solving 18:
"I'll hide it!"

Big Red has had a bad day at school and has a note from his teacher. He doesn't want to show it to his mother because he knows he will get into trouble. He's thinking of throwing it away. What should he do?

Think of your own solutions and then turn the page 46 to see if you found any of Wally's ideas.

Problem-solving 19: "I'm being left out."

Felicity hasn't been asked to a classmate's birthday party and she learns that most of the other girls have been asked. She's feeling very disappointed and sad. What should she do?

Think of your own solutions and then turn to page 46 to see if you found any of Wally's ideas.

Problem-solving 20:
"No one likes me."

Freddy has invited several friends home after school but everyone has had an excuse for why they couldn't come over. What should he do?

Think of your own solutions and then turn to page 47 to see if you found any of Wally's ideas.

Problem-solving 21:
"I'm really mad!"

Big Red has a fight in the school yard with other children because they won't let him play with them. What should he do?

Think of your own solutions and then turn to page 48 to see if you found any of Wally's ideas.

Problem-solving 22:
"They won't find out."

Oscar steals Wally's baseball glove because his parents won't buy him one. He's hidden it under his bed. What should he do?

Think of your own solutions and then turn to page to 49 see if you found any of Wally's ideas.

Problem-solving 23:
"He's bothering me."

Felicity Feelings is sitting next to Oscar who keeps bothering her by touching her hair and kicking her under the desk. What should she do? If that doesn't work what should she do next?

Think about your own solutions and then turn to page 50 to see if you found any of Wally's ideas.

Problem-solving 24:
"I'm the best."

Freddy Feelings has started at a new school and in order to make friends he bragged to his classmates that he was a super basketball player but actually he has never played. His friends want him to teach them how to play. What should he do?

Think about your own solutions and then turn to page 51 to see if you found any of Wally's ideas.

Problem-solving 25:
"He threw it at me."

Molly is eating her lunch in the school cafeteria and one of her classmates throws food at her. What should she do?

Think about your solutions and then turn to page 52 to see if you found any of Wally's ideas.

Problem-solving 26: "It's a foul."

Freddy Feelings and Big Red are playing soccer with some of their classmates. They're on different teams. Freddy kicks the ball into the goal for what he thinks is the winning point. However, Big Red and his teammates argue that there was a foul. What should Freddy do? What should Big Red do?

Think about your solutions and then turn to page 53 to see if you found any of Wally's ideas.

Problem-solving 27:
"They're bullying me."

There are some kids at Freddy's school who are always teasing him - especially on the playground. They call him names, say nasty things about his mother, and take his lunch sometimes. One of the kids threatens him that his older brother will beat him up if he tells anyone. He's afraid to walk home after school because sometimes they go after him and take away his book bag and hurt him. What should Freddy do?

Think about your solutions and then turn to page 54 and 55 to see if you found any of Wally's ideas.

Problem-solving 28:
"They won't let me play."

Several girls are playing hopscotch in the playground. Molly wants to play with them but they have excluded her and told her she can't play with them. What should Molly do?

Think about your solutions and then turn to page 56 to see if you found any of Wally's ideas.

Solutions

Problem 1

Solution: Ask a friend for help.   **Solution:** Admit mistake.

Problem 2

Solution: Congratulate yourself.   **Solution:** Stay calm.

Problem 3

Solution: Tell yourself to keep trying.

> I'M NOT A QUITTER. I HAVE TO KEEP TRYING AND IT WILL GET EASIER SOME DAY.

Solution: Tell your teacher about your difficulty.

> I HAVE DIFFICULTY WRITING AND SPELLING.

> MANY CHILDREN DO FIND IT HARD. EVERYONE LEARNS AT A DIFFERENT PACE. LETS TRY TO LEARN JUST A FEW WORDS FIRST.

Solution: Ask for help.

> DO YOU KNOW HOW TO SPELL THE WORD DINOSAUR?

Problem 4

Solution: Ask for a turn.

Solution: Wait.

Solution: Do something else.

Problem 5

Solution: Tell the teacher.

Solution: Be loyal to your friend.

Problem 6

Solution: Share your feelings.

Solution: Offer to help.

Problem 7

Solution: Wait and watch.

Solution: Ask to take a turn.

Problem 8

Solution: Be a good sport.

Solution: Pay a compliment.

Solution: Say what you feel.

Problem 9

Solution: Throw away frustrated feelings.

Solution: Apologize.

Solution: Offer to fix it.

Problem 10

Solution: Be loyal to your friend. Speak up.

Solution: Speak up for yourself.

Problem 11

Solution: Say No! - Have confidence in what you know is right.

Solution: Ask the teacher.

Problem 12

Solution: Say how you feel.

Solution: Ignore them.

Solution: Distract yourself.

Solution: Throw away bad feelings.

Solution: Use humor.

Problem 13

Solution: Ask for help.

Solution: Make a plan and congratulate yourself.

Problem 14

Solution: Stay calm.

Solution: Apologize.

Problem 15

Solution: Tell the truth.

Solution: Think positive thoughts.

Problem 16

Solution: Apologize.

Solution: Ask for help.

Problem 17

Solution: Offer to share.

Solution: Offer to trade.

Solution: Offer to take turns.

Problem 18

Solution: Have courage.

Solution: Think about better times ahead.

Problem 19

Solution: Be brave.

Solution: Do something that makes you feel happy.

Problem 20

Solution: Practice helpful thoughts.

Solution: Make another plan.

Problem 21

Solution: Imagine yourself in your shell,
and take three breaths.

Solution: Walk away.

Solution: Relax.

Problem 22

Solution: Admit you've done wrong.

Solution: Forgive yourself.

Problem 23

Solution: Tell him to stop.

> PLEASE STOP KICKING ME. IT'S BOTHERING ME. THANK YOU.

Solution: Move away.

Solution: Reward yourself for staying calm and for ignoring trouble.

> I'M NOT GOING TO LET HIS KICKING ME GET ME UPSET. I'LL IGNORE HIM. I'M DOING WELL AT STAYING CALM. HE'LL SOON STOP.

Problem 24

Solution: Admit your mistake.

Solution: Praise other kids.

Problem 25

Solution: Ignore it.

Solution: Tell the teacher.

Solution: Tell him to stop.

Problem 26

Solution: Be a good sport.

Solution: Be a good loser.

Solution: Have a calming thought.

Problem 27

Solution: Take charge and tell your parent/guardian.

Solution: Tell yourself it is right to tell on someone who is hurting you or someone else.

(Problem 27 continued)

Solution: Disobey the bully but don't fight.

Solution: Avoid bullies and stay close to someone in authority.

Problem 28

Solution: Take no for an answer.

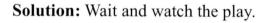

Solution: Wait and watch the play.

Solution: Try again.